Dear Blackbird,

THE AGHA SHAHID ALI PRIZE IN POETRY

Dear
Blackbird,

JANE SPRINGER

THE UNIVERSITY OF UTAH PRESS
Salt Lake City

THE AGHA SHAHID ALI PRIZE IN POETRY

Series Editor: Katharine Coles
Advisory Editor: Peter Covino

 The Defiance House Man colophon is a registered trademark of the
University of Utah Press. It is based upon a four-foot-tall, Ancient
Puebloan pictograph (late PIII) near Glen Canyon, Utah.

11   10   09   08   07   1   2   3   4   5

LIBRARY OF CONGRESS CATALOGING-IN-PUBLICATION DATA

Springer, Jane, 1969-
 Dear Blackbird / by Jane Springer.
     p. cm. — (Agha Shahid Ali Prize in Poetry)
  ISBN 978-0-87480-897-1 (pbk. : alk. paper)
  I. Title.
  PS3619.P757D43 2007
  811'.6—dc22

                              2006039275

Cover image © Pete Starman/Riser/Getty Images

To the memory of
Mary Brown Springer (1936–2004)

Contents

Dear Blackbird,

The crows maintain that a single crow could destroy the heavens.
There is no doubt of that, but it proves nothing against the heavens,
for heaven simply means: the impossibility of crows.

—Franz Kafka

Dear Blackbird,

Last night I drank to the measureless arc of you—your body's black rivermark over the levy.

If there was a sound at all in the night then it was as the dog's fencehowl splintered off from a chorus of running loose hounds.

If there was a thought it was the brittle dry husk of a thought's discontent at containment & of its leaning toward a new frost.

If there is a motion I've memorized its slight idiosyncrasies: The glitch in the loop of the root underfoot—

rain leaving one swath of light to mark the way of your flight through this field.

Toward what heaven or abyss do you go—lead by the dry inkwell of one blighted eye, the good one stocked with such stolen grain.

What your wings know—eclipsing them both. Your wings, eclipsing the moon.

I do not say that I wished to go with you—
I do not say that I wished to go with you—

> Truly as was & as
> ever will be
> yours—
>
> *Scarecrow*

Nostalgia

Whenever I see white horses I think of Jenny
    who never let us get too close or, when we

did, tricked her way out from our braided sage
    ropes & vanished behind the sawdust heap

or tin-roofed shed, as though we might forget
    she was loose on the town again. & how if

we saw her—it was only in parts: Her ethereal
    hooves encrusted in mud below the old hay

truck or ears atop towering buckets or tail wisps
    out from a barreled wall of grain. & how

we theorized on where she might have gone &
    some of us thought she grew translucent wings

& some us thought she was just an equine bitch
    for leaving while we had to stay—even if it

was raining & time to go home. Afterall, we had
    better chores to do than to catch a loose horse:

Mates to finalize & funerals to compose. & how it
    took us all—rapt in a séance to *call her up*: The

feckless ghosts of our eyes rolled back, muscles
    tuned to ninja-pitch & ears entranced for an odd

sonance we'd know once we heard it: Knocking an
    aluminum bin or falling with a thud from the loft

above, or rustling in with a ligature of leaves fresh
    played in the threshold of an erstwhile open door.

For the Appaloosa Who Never Took Sugar

Have you often dreamed of ditching
  the rider who cleaved to your motion—
    spent ends of her crop held taut as the

tenth bounced check at your neck, her
  heel jutting into the space between ribs—
    Woes! bleeding out from her straight

black jacket of corrupted accounts. No
  wonder you charge the goldenrod plain
    with mercurial speed before switching

    direction, impetuous beast—

    now rapturing toward a stand of iron
  trees where you will freeze. Since you
came we've found two riding boots dis-

    enfranchised from their feet & six hats
  blown free at the edge of the woods,
where you brazenly became a stunted

    Pegasus—decidedly grown too

stone for the gods, too mad for wings.

Broodmare

To begin with she grazed with the bliss of a horse who
     has emptied her pockets of all trailers & reins

        to journey no more except on the scent of sawdust
          & orange blossom blowing in from the east.

The list of her mind:

          bare back
          good mud
          pearl sky

Later this day, she will be bred to an inexperienced stud
     who'll accidentally mount her head resulting in

        a pulled neck muscle for her & hoof gashes across the
          chest for him. Her eventual foal will be born dead

                & delivered by a chain.

Still she will have no thought of:

          angels or
          slitting her own wrists
          I'd like to believe her grief will be good & done—

having nothing to do with the bridle of faith. But now
     a flatbed of fresh alfalfa & hay pulls into the paddock.

       & here, a white bird sits on the mare's back all day to catch
         biting flies. Come November, a cold snap will please her.

The differences between us:

        forelock & fetlock
        time & tense
        no hell girded under the heft of a three-tiered cake—

(Then, too, she can see past the grounds to a field where the gate is ajar.)

Whisper

That summer the barnboy wore a backwards hat & belted his jeans with a
   shoestring. He had snake eyes—dice rolling ones everytime—

not every bad man is unlucky—

  & if he'd been a band he'd have been the sort to piss on the
audience, or to bite off batheads then toss their
           bodies into the blue stagelights.

There are horses with the god gone out of them.

   Whisper was manewild, scarmuscled—the kind of horse one does
not challenge to a straight pool match.

   When we passed carrots like love letters through the slats to him,
back then, he flattened his ears &
       stormed the barn door.

There are horses with the god gone out of them.

   That barnboy had enough baling strength to keep a girl corpsed in
his grip against the splintered tackroom floor—as tobacco
          floated like tealeaves

  from his mouth into her mouth & whoever she was,
she lost her name that year, same as the summer girls before her.

We long dreamed of loving the holiness back into Whisper—

      Afterall, we were young & full with the mean desire to gentle &
mend horses from their coal-blitzed eyes & ash-breath down
                                    to their fine-split hooves.

      Even so—Whisper broke one of our shoulders with a single
bite as we turned our backs to shovel his waste
                          & line his bed with clean sawdust.

When that barnboy bragged he knew how to show a horse who's boss & slid
      a chain over Whisper's nose to lead him,
                        Whisper reared

& flung him so he seemed a rodeo clown, tied at the hands—back bent &
      suspended in air as dust above the cloudless paddock—

This went down while we laughed & ate lunch on a tailgate—
                        Fucker got what was coming.

An Aubade for Sebastian & Marnie

If a horse has something of a man in him
then Sebastian wore the zippered
jumper his grandfather gave him, flourish

of oilrag hung from one pocket, handsome—
he must have been the last, wan
attendant in America to insist on pumping

women's gas. Each night we latched him
in his stall—& by daybreak he stood
nose tipped to the palomino, Marnie, who

did not think of herself as fat—but fat/sexy
like the platinum actress who wasn't
ashamed to have herself sewn into evening

gowns & who often played dumb, yet had the
sense at her audition, to saw the heel
of one shoe down to give her gait more swag—

He could have nosed himself into the tack
        room instead—rollicked in oats.
            He could have tested his time on the dirt

      racetrack or lolled in Arcadian pasture, those hours.

But having till firstlight to think it over,
he walked to the stall three doors down, as the

moon, in its saffron garment, left, & the first birds
rose in morning song. This is how I
remember dawn: Two uncommon horses, locked

in silhouette—*love*—despite the daily barn coming on.

Why Bother Resurrecting the Dead

When their multitudes of affliction may better serve
a second earth,

that needs more haunting through its branches—
needs more briar, less water &
more apology. Even

the weeping cherry seems less romantic, now,
having blossomed tiny handkerchiefs
& cast them down—

it belongs to the realm of barn-born kings & the first-
born sons of Herod
(whose springs were silenced underground).

I have to believe that what I love is not wrapped up in
the finite magic of a discourse,
already drawn.

& that the first place is moving on, so that the
first word is not, finally, spoken, but
stays on the palate—

just as the sparrow stays among the palmetto fronds.
Not still,

or having any thought we think it should—
but warbling in ways we
have not known.

Lamentations

If you want to hear the stories about the sisters who thwarted chiggers
by rubbing coal oil on their arms & legs before wading into brambles, &
how they walked out of the forest with blackberries staining through the
upturned laps of their floursack dresses, on the fourth of July—do not
lament. I could have gone on

believing they would wash their hair in a rainbarrel, forever.

& that the mailman would bring live chickens in boxes, so they could
exchange eggs for groceries. That there would always be more eggs, because
they would trick the hens into perpetually warming their nests, by placing
glass replicas under them. Befriended chickens would run like dogs, through
the brooder, to greet them. Their mother said

her hell had been on earth, fighting with eight mouths over gravy scraps.

& even if it wasn't the quaint picture it seems now, still their mother was the
only one who could bring herself to break the necks of barnyard fowl. To
soak their bodies in salt, loosening the feathers, then to burn the down with
lit ends of a newspaper. So there was fried chicken wrapped in a towel to
warm the sisters' hands on the walk to school.

I could have gone on believing they would whet their knives on a stone.

& on Christmas, the oyster truck would arrive from the coast. So they
would go on riding in a buckboard to meet it, in Beech Grove, Kentucky.
They would circle the dolls they wanted in a Sears catalogue. Thread

cranberries & popcorn into garland. The neighbor would carry a violin on his back down a dirt road. I could have

believed they would keep milk cold by lowering it into the well, all summer.

Would wake before dawn to coldpack enough fruit for the next winter. Would slide their knives under thin-skinned peaches & slip the wet & delicious fruit into jars for hours, in a sweltering kitchen. Aching fingers & hump shouldered. Until a group of teens arrived in a car & tempted the girls to skinnydip in Green River. On the hottest

day of the year, one sister finished the other one's work & the other

sister went, sans socks & shoes, sans apron, to the other side of the bridge, where tent revivals were sometimes held. & long lines of believers waded, fully dressed, into the riverbed. Here John, the prince of Baptists, held a woman—waist deep—in his arms so that from the shore they seemed to waltz in her despair before he drenched her,

then brought her out again, her face—wet & ecstatic with sungilt grace.

It must have been the parting of their ways, the river—each sister, laying claim to one side of it. Each one believing she followed a chosen path: My aunt, still, coldpacking fruit in the sober kitchen of obedience. My wild mother, forgetting that place, because heaven was on earth.

Even now, unbuttoning her blouse & letting it fall through the clouds.

⁓

There must have been mornings when the mother dumped a warm basket of clothes over her baby. Pulled a sock over her hand & mouthed the language of puppets. Fresh scent of linens & new cut grass lollygagging on the spring sill of a screenless window where white cotton curtains spoke kindly of the visiting wind.

If it happened that way for mother & me, I could not remember it.

But I could picture my two older sisters, working beside us. Holding opposite corners of a pillowcase. Walking to the middle to kiss, because folding sheets is a kind of holiness that resides on the lips, for children. There must be thousands of ways to remake the past, which is why poetry is the science of opposites. Before she died,

our mother fretted for too often sleeping, but she might not have slept,

in her dreams. So many new mothers want to play piggies with their baby's toes instead of crying into their own pillows. Here I have made a space for mothers who wanted to bounce their babies on the bed, but didn't, because desire lives on its own accord, & regardless of circumstance. & because, whether they came to fruition or not—

my mother's desires move me, now, to pour laundry over my son. This is

a ritual he has come to expect, so he waits on the bed with outstretched arms. Even as the warm clothes tumble over him, my mother's unspent joy releases its atoms in the laughter of a baby, who could be anyone's—because holiness resides in the galaxy of wishes that reality only seems to exempt. Poetry is the science of forgiveness.

& if I & my sisters knew our mother was locked behind a door & weeping,

do not lament. She had planted whole beds of flowers to keep us company, in Prairie Grove, Arkansas. A field of yellow jonquils ran between our father's church & the manse—we never knew it was not our home. The rabbit's foot, on its reedy stalk, grew soft shoes in the late fall. & crocus pushed their prayerful hands through the last snow. Eden is the garden

god set aside for children. & we grew up, planting rubber snakes between rows of blooming squash & marigolds. So that, at some undecided hour, a voice would rise up from the tomatoes to reveal its dark canals. (An aunt, say, whose pulled up skirt would release vegetables as she ran from the plaything we had hidden at her feet.) I am not saying we were not lonely.

A royal court of fading irises, caterpillars lolling on their tongues.

Evenings on the porch where we snapped the heads of captured beans & left their bodies in a bowl. Or pulled corn husks away from their towers, so Rapunzel's locks, free & silken as the evening sunlight, slipped through our hands to the floor. Looking out on the apple tree whose overburdened branches were tied with buckets to catch ripened fruit.

I don't know what it is about sex & death, but the days when my aunt & mother slept as children, in the same bed or under the stars, together, are gone. & even then, they fought to keep their bodies alone, at rest, by drawing invisible lines between themselves—before the candles were one by one, blown out.

After we bury her under a forest of canopied trees, my father wants to talk

about how, in Keokuk, Iowa, his bride made love to him for the last time standing up against a wall until, on the other side of it, pots & pans shook from their shelves, forever. How she was a demon in the sack, & scorched the brim of his minister's hat. Or how they made love too loud, while rooming in an old woman's house, & probably

that is why she evicted them, because it reminded her of widowhood.

He speaks of their love this way, exuberant & eternally naked. Which is how she wanted to remember it, too, after she lost use of her legs. & the two divided beds & eventually rooms that seemed to span separate sides of the

house, in Tallahassee, Florida. Cancer does not love to sleep, or to share a
bed, but wants a room to itself. This is the way

darkness keeps to itself, its own room of disappointments & dreams—

the owl awake, the cock asleep. The morning glory twisting up the telephone
pole & closing the purple shades of its many mouths, till daybreak. The
phosphorescence tossed on the gulf waves, until the last of the lit shrimp
boats have met the dawning shoreline. Night has its own reality, apart from
day. Which is why

poetry is the science of dusks & dawns. I'll tell you the truth just once:

Whitman kept all the sleepers to himself but one, & she wasn't just a demon
in the sack. When she wasn't sleeping by daylight, she was the demon
slinging a house shoe at her children over the front seat of the Plymouth
while simultaneously steering it between the orgasmic, careening semis &
Beetle Bug Blue, Piddiddle, Beetle Bug Black.

Not a fluffy sex kitten, our mother, not a creampuff, not even romantic.

Except in the way a natural disaster, i.e. an earthquake/volcano/hurricane, is
romantic when it has already passed away, leaving a wake of uprooted trees,
strewn bodies, & whole stores of broken plates for survivors to clear away.
Jesus, her temper was magnificent. Beds—even when she was well, she left
them to eradicate nocturnal dust. If the trunks

of the longleaf pines seemed bent, then she straightened them with her ax.

& if my father's cornbread pans could not contain the batter's drip, she
buried them in the back yard. (Our father worked with a modicum of
cookware.) If there were neighborhood hounds kept penned, she broke their
gates & urged them to form packs along the levees of those rivertowns we
moved from. I remember

my father, naked, except for grandmother's quilt, clutched to his chest

as he fled down Thirty-fifth Street, past docile families sipping milk on their moonlit porches—mother pursuing him with a soup pan in one hand & a rolled up newspaper in the other. & who wouldn't *rather* remember making love with such a woman, who, for me, will always be running after her husband shouting *Bastard! Horse's Ass!* It must have

been like making love, all at once, to the seven maids of Pleiades, on crack.

My father, my favorite artist: It must have been like making love to chaos, until the sun & moon went haywire & the planets shifted into alignment. Do not lament, it is what we do so much these days since she is gone— make love to chaos. Not one amongst us afraid, anymore, to examine the teeth of that lion.

In the Afterlife of Clothes

Six siblings & two parents
   divided by one man's wage,
equals two rooms & three beds.

My father slept between his
   brothers & his father's razor
strap. Some summers he slept

in his uncle's washtub where
   his eighteen-year-old aunt asked,
Where would he like to touch?

My mother slept in a field when
   the boards of her house swelled,
there were no electric fans

on tobacco farms, in Kentucky,
   then. Her sheets lilted over
her body with each June wind.

After they married, our parents
   slept under quilts their own
mothers patched from discarded

clothes, & so their families never
   left them alone: But here,
a brother's sleeve would reach

across their twin-breathed chests,
   as though to pass salt over a
crowded table. The dead never

do keep their hands to themselves—
       & even stillborns'
empty hems cradled their toes.

Quilts in a Pattern of Flower Gardens

Our grandmother cut
her patterns from
brown paper sacks then fit

flowers the size of
camels through
her nimble-swift needle

& Lord, what do you
think of that
thimbleful of miracles?

Where each face of the flower was composed
of the same six-faceted shape—honeycomb,
our expression. Angular. In this way we wore

the bedclothes of that other generation. Aprons—
one for every weekday. Workshirts from the
shipyards of World War II. Black widowsuits.

Our first beds, pulled out drawers of cedar chests
lined with wrap from gifts already opened. Wood
slats lining our backs. Mad desire for polka dots.

The rifle above the door.
The sign in the window for ice.
The lye in a cauldron of lard.

The well in the woods.
The basket of fabric.
The rifle above the door.

The ways three becomes four. Three words,
for instance, stitched together with *and*—the Lord in three persons &
I, with my ear to the other side of the door, not knowing
the fourth daughter existed (just long enough) to get herself born.

The way four flower garden quilts were thought of—
but only three pieced with a visible seam—the other one webbed with
invisible thread that stayed in the attic of grandmother's hands.

Let us take it out & have a look, yes—it is just like ours:

Three undulating borders & the fourth border straight as the
bridge between rivers. Three borders pretty, to see to see, to
enclose the body. The fourth border a demarcation for her sleepyhead.

Had we delighted in fevers—what kept us from chores?

Pocked, measled, stillborn.

Cotton batting raise the plane, swell in the pores
of those petals. On the line, I love to dry in the sunlight—

fluttering by goldfinches fatted on ryegrass.

If by Chance You Meet Three
Small Town Southern Girls

I.

A CAUTIONARY TALE: THE MIDDLE SISTER

She was green & greener than anything I have seen in the South which says
      something of how even moss unfurling down the Ozark mountains
lacked luster when compared with the naiveté of middle sister. If you asked

her she would say that after a rain she took off her shoes every time to run
      outside & that she was a horse with a real horse name & her legs in
the wild wet grass were strong as the last of the mustangs that have, this

month, come to auction. Perhaps—what stunted her galloping—the
      omnipresence of trees & breathless envelope of mist or horse apples
rolling underfoot. The way the sun neither rose nor set except in the space

between leaves. It has been suggested the shoot em' up black & white flicks
      & books about horses were too romantic or at least went on too
long—& if only her parents had burned *Black Beauty* & *National Velvet* she

might not have moved out West where the potted yucca plant blew from the
      balcony during a dust storm, crushing her car. Or where the butcher
bird skewered lizards on barbed wire fences & shrilled: *I'll be back for you, later*

across the flat land, dotted with pump jacks, reeking of oil. Searing the backs
      of migrants then sweeping the footprints out from under them. The
place where letters whirl in to be stamped by nobody's hand: Return to

sender. If you asked she would say she worked as a second grade teacher &
      she wore second grade teacher clothes & reared two children who were
not her own & she loved two people who did unspeakable things.

& you wouldn't know she barrel-raced.

Out West there were ways to train horses by wielding on them a forty pound
        chain. Or by roping their legs & leaving their bodies all night in the
dark under a tarp or wool blankets depending on which was on hand.

One: (She won't say his name), cocaine taped under the sink. Burning house.
        Insurance money. A smiling gash that ran like freight the length of
his neck. The second one: Prostitutes, written on slips. Gun leveled at his

brain or pointed akimbo. It took twenty years to get out of that place & if
        you asked her she would say she never gets angry because of the time
when she was twenty & the temper, what little temper she had, was beaten

out of her. She never drew on the walls or bit anyone & her second grade
        teacher warned not to let this child grow up without learning how to
be mean, which happened, anyway. Still, you should see how she edges her

weight to one side—to turn a horse, without reins.

II.
NOTES ON THE ELDEST'S LAST BIG PRODUCTION

Here was the set where I lived with her for two months & where her
husband shot a rat out from under the couch & there was the steel table
where she said her husband's father tried to rape her during a
complimentary exam.

Since we last spoke, I've had a baby.

I wanted the father-in-law recast—lacking as he did the skills of
intimidation that equine veterinarians notoriously lack. How could those
hands (handsomely used to gentling horses) so brutally force an actor of her
stature into—

We should have done lunch & talked it over.

The movement where her mother-in-law chased her with a butcher knife, through the woods seemed cliché. Perhaps if she had domesticated the pursuit? Opted for a more limited space—say, the broom closet. This may have "amped-up" the tension—though it would have made for a more difficult escape. I wanted to say, to the actress:

What if she caught you instead.

I wanted to tell her to ax the neighbor with the poisoned mustard. She was less credible than the middle sister plotting to rub her out by mailing her a salmonella-esque Christmas turkey. (See, how by contrast, this made the mustard seem generic.)

Her decision to cut me—I hoped was not permanent. Her script seems implausible without me—a lizard who'd lost her tail,

I could not scale the window without looking back.

Still, it seemed too coincidental that all of the women in her piece wanted her dead & that all of the men in her piece wanted her prostrate & naked across a steel table. With the exception of dad. Who wanted her how she was—mowing her name in the grass—

The things I can't say

that, nevertheless, began when she shoved chopsticks up her nose to ruin every family photograph & ended

not yet.

He was crucial to the part she gave him. Having loved her the most, he had the most to lose when she said: Goodbye, & meant: With this madness, I will ruin you. & even if it was just a handful of scenes from a gothic script—

still the fact we were poor & he was a minister made America want to
    believe

(god is dead) his role in her production.

I pray that all of the scenes with her own children were kept. Especially the
one where the eldest walked from the sandbox to see the larger than life
portrait of St. Michael slaying the dragon that she—

her hair with white flowers, her brushes in coffee cans—

is still, in my mind, painting across the face of that trailer, so prettily set
under the live oak. There was such detail, in the dragon—each scale drawn
plump & decadent as a pound of flesh—more or less. How at once I loved
her daughter's star-struck expression when she said,

O Mommy! It's Beautiful.

III.

THE BABY IN FRONT

I am tired of being always last—for I, too, have
        bundled my Cinderella panties & three saltine
            crackers into a kerchief before hobo-ing past the

vaulted cemeteries & heroines tied to rusted
        tracks (no one missed me)—as if I were the *Z*
            incarnate of some outdated alphabet. I—from the

heart of the heartwood, in the casket of descending
        numbers—have dropped just as much acid as the
            other two before me, then dissolved into Georgia

O'Keeffe flowers until the facade of the bleak &

tormented towns that surrounded me & my sisters
gave way to the red enormous sundown beauty of

the shimmering clitoris. Boys at my door—boys
holding peaches & open umbrellas & gold carpet
promises for no more tornadoes gathering at my feet—

I am tired of being always last & wanting the
clothes from my sisters' closets, & running to get
caught up with the kisses & oohs & aahs leveled

gunlike at my sisters' beauty. If you want me, tell
me you know not what other women I speak of. Tell
me if you saw my sisters without their collars you'd

call Beast Recovery. Say it would take as much heroin
as there are tacky plastic flamingoes in Florida for you
to consider my sisters beautiful as they are & tell me

you will have no other gods besides myself before
you. & if either of my sisters asks you what I said about
them, just tell them *It ain't nobody's business but my own.*

Remind me again how the lame shall enter first, then
dress my handmedown wounds & I will throw myself
in front I will throw myself in front of a train for you.

Words

I almost died once.
                    You wouldn't have known it.

With a hymnbook in
                    your hands & a coffin of my favorite color on order

you still, couldn't have
                    planned it. That is what the survivors mean when

they say it happened so
                    quickly. While you marveled over my newborn—

record of weight,
                    measuring tape, navigating his head—

hands pressed
                    to the glass of the new room of

his new breath.
                    I froze in the white light

of hospital lamps
                    & my body

shook out
                    what tremors

the living have.

When I trembled
            like that again, it was by the porchlight

of your last night—
            as though my body had known what I had not guessed

& I left both my love
            & infant in bed to hear the water rising in your lung,

overcome your worldly
            songs—which were so plain (on the day I

almost died) to ask on
            sight of my half/dead body, had anyone

thought to feed the
            dog (a verse omitted from the Psalms).

That night I would
            have burned the Psalms

to hear your
            ordinary voice raised

in questions
            so ill suited

to circumstance.

God is so small
         as to weld himself to the warp & woof of

the glasses I took
         because they were the last thing besides my face that

touched your face—
         that morning you died. & I knew why the *quick*

were named for the
         living in the apostle's creed—not so much

for speed of foot as
         for the smallest wooded thing, such as

a splinter piercing
         the *quick*—most tender part of the

nail. & here I
         want to say, it's not the

sun's eventual
         burning out, but

it's burning
         in the first

improbable place.

St. Augustine wound
        past the blighted *I* of his confessions

to get to Genesis—
        no proper end, its root meaning: To beget—& yet

otherwise: To know.
        Christmas here is a murder of ornaments & phonecalls

without you at the other
        end. The advent reading comes from John the

Baptist who admits:
        I am not the Messiah. Neither is he Elijah or the

prophet, & all
        he can say for himself is: *I am the voice*

of one crying in
        the wilderness. His purpose:

Pointing to
        what love takes

shape outside
        the sole

estate of being.

I hardly believe
            the child in me did not die when I gave

birth to another being,
                        much less when I clung to your already vacant

body—but pushed a
                    boulder of grief aside, & tears have never come so

freely nor wisdom fled
                        alongside all omniscience. Though you may

never lose your glasses
                        again, neither may you know I wear them,

as I did when playing
                        dress up. My hearing improves,

if not my sight—
                & begs presence when

your grandson
                asks: Shall we

walk in the
            woods where

the birds sing?

Here is the wing
           to match the last, to strike the last, to burn

the last, by the time
           it reaches you—there will be nothing but plumage

breaking away from
           all the words of it. That's why you are wherever you

are & I am here—to say
           these things. A friend once said the soul is

bright like this: & struck
           a hammer to the pavement, loosening

sparks from it. I
           think he may have got it wrong &

the soul cannot
           be seen or heard or held or

comforted, yet
           here it is: Cloudshift,

rejoicing at
           the center of

all absence.

Dear Blackbird,

The first summer after you left rolled in as a white & fine-grained fog. The question became not: Where had *you* gone—but one of location, nevertheless, behind what curtain:

The little farmhouse, its sputtering truck & tin shed. The field where trysting lovers met. The dissolution of it all.

& I in a shrunken, hangdog coat. Eternal straw & soddenly present.

Then came a clamor of birdsong, returning:

Grackle, eagle, wild turkey. The silvery voice of a thrush in the thicket. Mockingbird perched on a branch by the highway. Each song brilliant. No song abiding—

it is not, so much, your image I miss.

But neither the farmer nor his wife nor you, Blackbird, came to restore me. So come, hail & damnation. Come, anyone. Come, wind. When the crows descended, I welcomed them.

That is how I became a heaven for crows, by loving their footfall on my shoulders. So learning the language of crows & bidding them: Come, stay, eat.

I wish I could tell you then, you would not find the corn in ruins, my trodden form in a heap by the ditch—

but that is what becomes of one who makes an Elysium of grief.

The second summer you were gone sprang from a reclamation of weeds banded round my clothing & always this dream:

I am chaff lilting slightly over a swift & stoneworn creek & from here I have only one thing left to ask: What part of me—were you?

Truly as was & as
ever will be
yours—

Scarecrow

Sestina for Being Born
Into a Fairytale Ending

Accept all the rules that apply: your mother must die
        & you must be grievously vexed by your kind—
though I cannot tell you if they will have one or three eyes,
        much less if they will be sisters or brothers who turn
into swans or crows, who live in a glass house by
the moon. Either way you must come to know the woods

in uncanny ways—walking all day in wooden
        shoes in search of berries that should be dead
but instead spring from the frozen ground. & by
        the grace of god you will find kindred
rivers—each bidding you drink—but you will turn
into a bear or fawn if you do. Your eyes

will suffer home, but you'll sooner walk through the eye
        of a button than find it here, where the wood
petrifies in the form of faces & hermits turn
        goldsmiths & broom makers alike to stones which die
to be spoken to, or recognized by a kindred
soul passing through in ravishing motion. Goodbye

you will say to the stones as you touch them. Goodbye
        you will say to the mother of your voice, & your eyes
will drop gold coins in splendid grief that is kindred
        somehow, more with the mountain—more with the woods
& their manifold passages through time & death
than with the brothers & sisters you left turning

in their own changeling beds. In their absence you'll turn
            more witty, pretty, or handsome on the green byway
of each passing year. You will build a castle to die
            for from ash & become the huntsman, hitting the bullseye
every time—or spin a starry gown from the wooden
spindle bequeathed to you by unknown kin—

a magic aunt, perhaps, who has worked with a kinship
            of birds to keep the good & sorrowful turns
in your life evened out—you are not out of the woods
            yet. Now you must cut the giant who sleeps by
the hillside to ribbons before it opens its eyes
of wrath on your future love, who will *without you*, die.

Are you sure you want this wooded life, these kindred
            spells handed down from death & love's return?
                    Wait by the well. *This will be tragic.* Shield your eyes.

For the Love of Turkey Vulture #2

When I was twenty-two I stayed for a year in the forest—it wasn't a
      metaphorical forest with a river of dreams running through it,
it had coordinates & a name but the name was so silly I can't even say

it, you would not take me seriously if I did. It wasn't the forest of fairy-
      tales either, there was no trail of half-eaten breadcrumbs, no fox
tricking crow out of his brie & certainly no witch invited me into her

kitchen for cocktails. I boiled nettles for tea. I dug up Jerusalem artichokes
      & mused mightily over how much they tasted like potatoes except
without butter or sour cream they tasted more like dirty roots.

After a week when the novelty of beef jerky & boiled greenery had worn
      thin, I wished for a fox or even a crow turning on a spit. It would
take months before I would consider acorn casserole a la grilled

children. There were things besides old women with pointy shoes to be
      scared of, for instance the dried up mouths of wells scarcely hidden
by leaves, & the vineclaimed houses that would go on

being ghosted by butterflies long after I had turned twenty-three. Rodents
      or bears, I couldn't tell which, continually brushed my tent at night,
which didn't scare me so much as an occasional random shotgun

blast & the thought of drunk hunters aiming for deer through the trees. I
      came to the woods to be free from fear—the year after I don't know
how many men pinned me down behind a gravel road bar

set beside a picturesque bayou. I came to the woods to learn how not to
      drink so many hallucinogenic things. Which is why I insist the forest
was real. There were no widegrinning pixies hocking

popcorn & pixiedust by the worn paths of animals & there were no
　　　succubae, topless, on the river's lawn. There was just me in my bug-
bitten skin, rancid jeans & t-shirt. I boiled water took care of my

teeth & bathed with a cloth dipped into a saucepan—in this way the weeks
　　　spread like one gaping yawn of unincredulousness to the next. Which
is another way of saying that year was so boring & sober

& sexless that the occasional encounter with an errant orange mushroom
　　　growing out of a tree trunk warranted orgasm. The moon was more
vacant than silver. The tree leaves were gone or green with scant

months of technicolor in between. The paths were rust orange & the river
　　　waxed brown. The rain the rain the frozen tent poles. The only
miraculous piece of the year occurred on the day I had

packed my things to leave—& had to do with one turkey vulture colliding
　　　midair with another on what looked like the way to dinner. The
crash was cartoonish by nature the only thing missing—two

bubbles floating over their heads & filled with black asterisks. Though now
　　　I recall a childhood cat tricked into a bathtub in pursuit of a cousin's
flashlight's beam—then it seemed every beast who was not

polished off by another lived a lucky life—accident free. One vulture lay in
　　　a dizzy heap. One vulture recovered to join the feast with her friends.

The Island of Forgetting is Uncharted

Yet in the rucksack of every Sam Cooke-ified soul,
it is palpable as the afterscent
of gasoline or gingerbread—

I find it how I still expect to find morels, clothes
pinned to lines above the bed.
Or how I hear my late
lover's drawl, inked over my tongue.

& bedding down with Circe, here is where
Odysseus forgets his love, his wife,
his life, his home in Ithaca.

For on the Island of Forgetting, what existed long ago
becomes a clay pigeon for tiny
soldiers who take turns
blasting the features one remembers best:

Not Penelope's hands, but the way she held the hem
of her dress in her teeth
while descending the staircase.

Not his hair, but how my love kept wine canteened at
his hip, walking barefoot
through *The Garden of the Gods.*

O blue island of displacement, how I hate your ports
which hold little more than shacks
of ghosts grown fat
from the habit of absence.

Where one always asks, What did I come here for, this
field guide in my hand?

The Island of Forgetting has no records hall stacked
with romantic answers.

(Although, each morning one considers his bull-eared
shipmates hustling the trough
for scraps a kind of conclusion—
Still, if we *must* die, must we also be turned into livestock?)

The Island of Forgetting is a liar on the side of Poseidon,
who rearranges constellations

so that 444 Kelsey Street may as well be Cassiopeia. & if
I return to my love's door, still
it is with Kudzu, overgrown—

no one I know, now, looking out the crow's nest.

It is easy to leave—to wrestle a Cyclops, to wreck one's boat
on the Island of Forgetting.
The part of the story
one struggles to believe is Penelope's—

love wants a lawn where the torch stays lit for decades.

Love wants a woman who weaves a shroud each night
then rips the seams at dawn. Who
leaves her would-be lovers
slain where they feasted, in its void.

Boxes

Inside that box there was nothing but a bit
of someone,
leftover.

Blitzkrieg of mismatched worded magnets,
ions on the
fritz.

Cutoffs,
watermarked with riverswell.

Not unlike the other artifacts of self—

a child's clown, severed at the legs &
missing one
jinglebell.

It has taken one week to stop needing sense from the singular thing.

But since then, the rainbowed moon over Cumberland Gap has mixed itself
up with an overturned tricycle—where ice cream appears for those flinging
mown grass into spokes of a spun wheel. The night the law came into the
woods, Lemongrass went to jail for possession. & I never knew her honest
name, though her lover must have thought it as he wept, or kissed my hands.
Thunderclouds. O those tender pines—needleswept tent.

Why is the last in a series of tissue-wrapped objects always fraught?

For instance, this
cutting board.

 IV

A satisfied soul tramples on the honeycomb,
But to a hungry soul every bitter thing is sweet.

—PROVERBS 27:7

The Very Best Woman in All the World

—after Seth Tucker's "The Very Best Man in All the World"

The very best woman in all the world
auditions for Juliet's part.
But blinded by spotlights

on the silver gilt balcony, she leans too
far out over the set &,
hand over heart, plunges

into the orchestra pit. That is the way
of answering love letters
voiced up from the dark—

one is reminded how, accidentally,
symphonies end in a tangle
of broken-necked violins.

The very best woman in all the world
snorts coke at a party
for presidents. She is sexy

& wittier than she ever has been—yet,
troutlike, the sale tag still
hangs from the glittering

stream of her dress. That is the way of
making revolutionary
conversation—one is

reminded how it is most impressive,
coupled with a visual aid.
All of which is to say that

the very best woman in all the world,
while shocking &
mysterious, lacks repose. O,

she knows the knife-blade should face
the plate, & place cards
are, anyway, for those who

forget which dogs they'd rather have dinner
with—the dullard who
forgets her own name. Still,

she could do better than this—to have one
thumb on a thunderbolt,
one wheel in the ditch,

an eyeful of obscenely bright gemstones.
A book of digressive maps
depicts all the old roads

she has taken, mistakenly, while wondering
at Holsteins dressed, prettily,
up to their knees in Queen

Anne's lace. An admirable salad, if not
admirably eaten by roadside
cows who prefer a more

digestible grass, water from a plain lake.
That is the way of spiraling
into grace, & relative

unimportance. One is reminded how grand
the gesture of waking up is,
in a silent vault—when you

only meant to play dead long enough for the
right love to kiss the gathering
moss from your mouth.

Sleeping with the Excavator

Though by standing barefoot on the recliner & digging your toes between
        the cushions you may come up with an antique coin & the good
pair of scissors which you, in a household war,

cussed him for losing—you may not recover one fine hair of his, to analyze.
        Neither may he stay crushed in the velvet lining of a drawer against
his special occasion g-string & the bottle of good

cologne gone sour. Yet you examine the letters to his exes that lay unsevered
        from old notebooks—surely he is foxholed in the links of adolescent
cursive—but all you find is a lot of *what's up,*

not much here jumbled among a band of plaintive *forevers* that can't seem to
        escape their college-ruled homes. Then looking past his gently
wavering lips & concrete fillings, at night, to search

the opened cave of his throat, where his vows to you first rose like a ritual
        hieroglyph to the palate—you may, for a glitch in the moment, think
you hear him kneeling in the sagebrush at your

feet again—until this scarcely audible presence is displaced by the beast who
        wracks his body gutturally with sleep. You plunder his shipwrecked
hands for maps of the man you married

but come away instead, with the faded ink feeling of sunsets already sunk so
        low they light the spirits of the underworld & are ecstatic there—
therefore refusing to come back into this world again.

How every prevailing moral seems a quandary laid to rest inside a tomb of
        disappointment. How each regret keeps its faith in former glory.
How, to you, the skeleton seems less

a body fled from—more a temple of bones.

Being superstitious, you smash all the ladders leaning against the
        neighborhood houses & keep the jar of umbrellas outside the door.
& so there is no mirror hanging in the house, but then

why would you check the cracks between your teeth for spinach when your
        mate has never proven less than deft at ferreting out what alters your
appearance in such ways as are unpleasant to

behold or be beholden of? You're at the breakfast table drafting blueprints
        for your former groom's forehead. You've drawn a portal at his
frontal lobe & plan to enter it in bed to ransack his

night visions for the man you have been missing now for years—

but with one fatal gaze he ruins your measurements. You pour another box
        of gravel into the skillet. He leaves, & turning towards the kitchen
window, you—with prismatic clarity—glimpse a giant claw

indelicately slinging back your coffee. Dirtclods rain around you when you
        blink. There are few conundrums that a hot bath & a drag race will
not solve, but this one is buried chiefly among them.

How well you understand there is no loss like looking back on the city you
        loved as even now you are leaving it. How well you understand
that fathoming the past is another miraculous way

                                        of lacing fingers with the sea.

This Maker's Apology for the Tinman

Like every other apology, this one begins with a tidy noose hitched over a
      rough hewn stage that's fit with a trap door for quick & mannerly
carting away of the leftover drum of your body:

It was a hot day in hell when you were made, flybodies littered the shelves—
      a rat on a gluepaper trap chewed its leg off in feeble, failed escape
from the shop of your design. I had only half

the materials & tools I wanted—the other half lay to waste in the trunk of
      the Plymouth. I'm not saying I had a heart for you then, tucked in
the coil of a jumper cable or rolling around, loose

as the oddball screw you needed to hold together what once seemed crucial
      but now is forgotten—it's just that I had the silly false whim &
gumption to want to make one for you. For I

was in love with a girl who wore a gingham dress, a checkered past—a girl
      in opium up to her eyeballs. The half the materials I had were tin.
The half the tools I had were an ax. The half

the wits I used were straw. The girl—half witch with an hourglass shape—
      crystal balls for breasts—would pass by the window calling for her
lost dog. Like every other apology from maker to

man—this one is fraught with the girl—who I would buy up every villa in
      munchkinland to find now. But then you were yet to be, & I was in
a manic hurry to get somewhere I don't know

let's call it The Emerald City of Unbridled Fame & Immortality. So what you
      might be became what the end of a gorgeous ball of string might be
for a cat or a bedridden aunt who surfs

for the answer to god in the afghan plans of local shopping channels. Your
            chest lay flat as a map of Kansas across my table & stood for the
flicker of genius that's had but half made

good on & half gone bad. I—with a wrench in the claw of my hand. Like
            every apology this one is full of excuses & too long too late a time in
coming. The girl had the voice of a cedar waxwing.

Her voice—a garland of simple lilies growing out from the side of a barbed
            wire fence. Her voice like a glistering dew-winged dove floating out
to a sinking ark with an olive branch

taped in its teeth. The ruined black castle of her voice whistling through a
            grove of appletrees. That is how I remember it I make no apologies
for remembering it so distinctly it called

to me many times, you might say cyclonically—it called to me from the
            rootcellar of my childhood & all of its unfulfilled anything. This
apology's not to you but for you, my barren expanse

my fatal flaw, my kettle's core of a failed imagination, Tinman, slate blank
            of a heart that you are. I spent my attentions on oiling your joints &
cocking your hat to match the angle of mine

while lengthening shadows stalked the shop, & outside the nimbus of each
            lightning bug along the street blazed from bright to midnight blue.
I am sorry. But for the felled trees in the score

of my foolhardy making of you—the vanishing girl & I should have got back
            the dog, spent the gold bricks, burned the bitch broom & gone
sliding down the dry-eyed side of the rainbow.

An Addict's Guide to Pregnancy

Consider it tragic.

Consider it cute & suburban with a fashionable doula on call.

Consider it while sulking barefoot on a low rent beach in a garish bikini
      with a cigarette dangling from one hand & the disapproving
looks shot from the elite & divine unpregnant.

Consider it license to eat anything you want: Iron, clay, oranges.

Consider it falling asleep. Fall asleep. Wake up & consider it, falling asleep.
      Consider it suspiciously—settling a land lassoed with no sylvan
memory, yet—

Read about dreams.
      Due to its apparent quality of shocking & continual release from
reverie—consider it incapable of being rendered as a dream.

Try to see it differently—this is called the last vestige of hope.

Consider not the fruit, blighted, but the blighted branch the perfect fruit
      falls from.

Consider Horse.
      Consider Snow.
Consider the barren expanse, hoofprints & cliff to follow.

Consider cinematic ways to lose it, such as: Falling down an indeterminable
      destiny of stairs.

Consider it on all fours, swollen uddered, & braying from inside a barn.

That's a start.

Consider it pre-liberation as shards of a glass ceiling sword through the dark
towards you. Then rewrite the declaration of independence across a
pillowcase, in needlepoint.

Consider dust collected in the innumerable empty cradles of a winerack.
Concede to hyperbole: There are in fact eight empty cradles.
Suddenly, the towels need bleaching. The carrots, blanching.

Consider the forlorn razor, the perpetual housecoat of it.

In the haunted house of foreboding:
The devastating, hour-long seconds.

The accidents, fetal, looming towards birth: The syntactical error of one eye
in the middle of its tiny forehead & a crowd of proofing doctors with
a) microscopes b) rejection slips c) zoo cages.

Don't stop there: Consider the cord cut neck, the ectopic, the premature.
The horned & cloven hooved.

The motorcycle wreck that, down the line, is sure to paralyze it. The mother
you will surely be will screw it up before coming to that.

It's not unlike writing.

But consider it without Aspirin or Prozac.

A host of unblanketed, shivering birches.

Console yourself with folic acid.

Consider the invader pushing the territories of your organs back &
     ambushing your arsenal of thought, daily.

& childhood—yours. & friends—yours. The gin hidden in a sock drawer—
     yours. Self pity & mortality—yours. Consider them hijacked:

Whittle it down to the essential: Panic attack.

Then consider the prehistoric egg & fish that met inside your body.

This is stranger than science.
     This is stranger than god on mushrooms.
This is stranger than One Hundred Years of Solitude, emerging.

     Here are only half of the things to think of.

Does your sense of smell wax stronger than that of a mating dog: How did
     it happen—you, superhuman, without ever knowing it—

& still, there is magic left to consider:
     A rebirth, sensual enough to move rivers.
A notion outside the preconceived.
     A coming on of love like daylight.

From the center of your reserves—

     The one who will break the bank of your wisdom.
The one who cries: Hold my feet in your hands.

     The one who finds the scent of: Your sweater, your matted hair &
all of you down to your crooked bones—intoxicating—is coming.

The Borrowed Wife

Before she came, & loving the pause between lovers as he did, he kept the
      apartment of his heart uncluttered & hung a permanent vacant sign
between his eyes but couldn't help dreaming of fried chicken.

The anonymous traffic of husbands gunned past him. Loving the lull
      between songs as he did, he only played the tracks between tracks &
did not bother to break the habit of tipping the complex laundress

all of his twenties. I'm going bankrupt, he said. Check me out, the wife
      replied. So he pulled her down from the highest shelf & fondled her
title, her dedication, her list of acknowledgments, & found her

fortune in his pocket. & so he stopped doing what one does while one waits
      for a wife to turn up: Lugging the mattress down cheap streets from
efficiency to efficiency. Scanning porn. Talking to plants.

Instead he: Got used to the silver-flecked dust settling between the blinds.
      Let whole concertos wind past the allegro & through the cough in
the audience, until they had played themselves out to applause

& the conductor—he could imagine—had measured out her last bow. The
      hours hung their hats by his door & he watched happily as they:
Dismantled his morning paper. Blunted the edge of his favorite razor.

Reset the heating & cooling. Fed the sad-eared blue stray raccoon.

She always leaves something: A gold earring. The shape of her mouth across
      a frosty window. Good knives. The rucksack of outlandish practical
jokes her husband does not know she keeps. Her own home—

is unfathomably small. She could never fit more than one shoulder in at a
          time. A tidbit's house, underground, stocked with mice who drink
Cosmopolitans & dream: Big band. Tall tale. Acres of brie.

But see how, by contrast, here she fits in the borrower's house as: The
          fridge that wants nothing but condiments. The matchbook drying
beside the winerack. An open shirt draped over a chair—

has its own air of loneliness. Meanwhile, a husbandry of clothes hangs in
          stiff rows across a closet. Everything else is askew in the borrower's
house. Everything is spacious & strange as the happiness of:

A sudden downpour. Dice hitting doubles. Lush poppies unfurled
          underfoot. Sheep fucking. The thousands of joules flaring out from
lightning. Wind distorting the trees. He loves her he loves

her he loves the errant things his borrowed wife leaves when she leaves:

The earring, once, a gypsy band, worn—unjangled across his nightstand. Her
          kissprints distilled in a morning fog. An applecore in repose on the
cuttingboard. The Lucille Ball of her perfume. & she loves

the way it makes her smaller to leave him with only half her things.

The husband is a figment of the imagination: Continually wearing a rented
          tux & clipping new boutonnières from the neighbor's garden. He
is as the mayfly who exists for 24 hours then dies

to be replaced with his identical self. He is everything that arrives on time
          & in his suitcase he stores enough glass slippers to fit anysized foot.
You will know him by his locks: Bronze.

You will know him by his horse: White. You will know him by his serious
        bones & his lingering scent of myrrh. You will know him in the
nude: With no hair on his chest & holes in his hands & feet.

You will know him by his propensity to move immovable stones. But you
        will not know him in a crowded jukejoint where he looks like
everyone else. & you will not know him in jail where he buries

his head in his hands. He is estranged from the world as it is: Its wilting
        birdsong. Its leaves, cashed in. Its wine poured out. Even so—he
can't help whistling & wondering where his wife has gone.

It's not that he misses her, exactly, but he doesn't feel himself without her.
        For one: The fish in the freezer won't stop multiplying. For two:
Lepers lining up on his doorstep to beg outrageous favors.

The husband wants peace. The husband wants self-generating carnations.
        The husband wants to break his own arms then to watch them
reassembling themselves. With depth of vision—he tries

to picture his wife but he cannot remember if she has one or two heads.

There is the place where everything that has been taken or left or lost is
        returned to—there is: The borrowed wife's musical jewelry box.
The borrower's childhood runaway dog. The husband's inlaid hand mirror.

There is the money & document you forgot on the hood of the car as you
        drove away. On top of the last piece of pie, there are your
grandmother's pretty aprons. Your father's fleeting good looks.

There is: The shamrock. The rainbow connection. The answer to the Stela
        of Paser. There are God & Allah arguing for the affection of Eve.
& there is Eve playing with the buttons of Darth Vader's missing lightsaber.

Here are the librarian's fiftieth pair of misplaced glasses. Here are your
         mistakes, basking in the margin of error. Here are Saturn's—the rest of
the rings—such ancient, forgotten love piled up in the middle of nowhere.

The borrowed wife becomes light as the frond of a fern growing from a tree
         branch. She is not so much the matter of infidelity as the matter who
morphs according to her surroundings, which is in itself

an infidelity of sorts—to: The silhouette. The shadow. The shape of things
         determined by their rising stars & vanishing moons. & so is delight
adjacent to response. & so she shifts. & so she gathers

the ocean in her dress then disperses it over: The soldiered hayfield. The
         rusted LTD cruising the craterpocked street. The call girl's receipts.
The lilac in the dooryard bloom'd—until the love you feel for

her becomes the act of borrowing that overwhelms the loss of everything.

Dear Blackbird,

The only thing that made sense was to fall in love with a carpenter who could build a house upside down out of straw & standing on one foot—

afterall, a scarecrow is just remnant stuffing for old clothes—it took a man like that to make of me, something new.

I am a house now, delicate timber to see through—you are the attic, fat with trunks enclosing:

Seven years of famine
Ithaca
The map disclosing which channel you & I are to arrive through.

Or else you are the attic soaked with light from one window & there are no trunks here— but a clean pine floor & one small, upright piano against the far wall.

For there is an attic in every blackbird.

For every skilled carpenter there is one house to be built upside down out of straw & standing on one foot.

Which explains why the attic opens out to a jungle of elephant ear & red orchids. I have never seen anything so rare

as what the love of a carpenter can do.

This is not a letter for rebirth. The carpenter & I made a son with skin & hair as dark & fathomless as you.

He walks beneath the evening & says: Look, Orion is wearing a new belt—
as if the very stars are, each night, new.

Which is something Ovid understood:

How wheat rising from a field may, in a single day, take on the form of
brothers who love—& yet by dusk, turn their swords on each the other.

Or how by the deception of dreams one kingdom falls & all the time in that
world is lost—

Blackbird, away with truth. No carpenter ever built a house that was not his
church.

There's a war outside & a fat new box of kleenex in my every pew—Come,
join us—for the body repairs itself & there is much worship & choiring
left to do.

> Truly as was & as
> ever will be—

Acknowledgments

Grateful acknowledgment is due to the editors of the following literary magazines where these poems or slightly altered versions of them either first appeared or are forthcoming.

AGNI: "Why Bother Resurrecting the Dead"; *The Chattahoochee Review:* "Dear Blackbird," (first in sequence); *The Cincinnati Review:* "An Addict's Guide to Pregnancy"; *The Cream City Review:* "Sestina for a Fairytale Ending"; *The Hayden's Ferry Review* (2005 AWP Intro Award): "The Very Best Woman in All the World"; *lyric poetry review:* "Words"; *The Southern Review:* "Quilts" (retitled "In the Afterlife of Clothes"), "Lamentations," and "The Borrowed Wife" (the last of these to appear in the Winter 2007 issue, "Writing in the South"); *The Sycamore Review:* "Dear Blackbird," (second in sequence), "Dear Blackbird," (final in sequence); *32poems:* "Boxes"; *Verse Daily:* "Quilts" (retitled "In the Afterlife of Clothes"), reprinted with permission. Thank you to Bret Lott and *The Southern Review* (and Cleopatra Matthis, judge) for awarding me the 2006 Robert Penn Warren Prize in Poetry.

Too many ways to count, thank you to the folks in the Florida State University Creative Writing Program in Tallahassee, Florida.

Thank you to all the fine folks (John, Morrison, Dad, Leslie, Ike, Charlene, Jimmy, David, Mark, Bob, Laura, Jen, Debbie, Matt, Seth, Ricky, Connie, Mike, Bill, Kate, and Glenda) who had a hand (i.e. leant me either money, genius, or both) in shaping this manuscript—for I cannot imagine having completed it without the help of each of you.

Thank you to Agha Shahid Ali who, Janet Burroway tells me, could cook and dance as well as he wrote and who had a wicked sense of humor, to boot.

And finally, to J.D. McClatchy, thank you.